Daisy, My Dad, and the Letter **D**

Alphabet Friends

by Cynthia Klingel and Robert B. Noyed

The **Child's World**

The Child's World

Published in the United States of America
by The Child's World®
P.O. Box 326
Chanhassen, MN 55317-0326
800-599-READ
www.childsworld.com

The Child's World®: Mary Berendes, Publishing Director

Editorial Directions, Inc.: E. Russell Primm, Editorial
Director; Emily Dolbear, Line Editor; Ruth Martin,
Editorial Assistant; Linda S. Koutris, Photo Researcher
and Selector

Photographs ©: Tim Davis/Corbis: Cover & 21; Corbis:
9, 13; C Squared Studios/Photodisc/Getty Images: 10;
Dex Images, Inc./Corbis: 14; Mark M. Lawrence/
Corbis: 15; David Young-Wolff/PhotoEdit: 18.

Library of Congress Cataloging-in-Publication Data
Klingel, Cynthia Fitterer.
  Daisy, my dad, and the letter D / by Cynthia Klingel
and Robert B. Noyed.
    p. cm. — (Alphabet readers)
Summary: A simple story about a child's favorite
activities introduces the letter "d".
  ISBN 1-59296-094-4 (Library Bound : alk. paper)
  [1. Dogs—Fiction. 2. Father and child—Fiction. 3.
Alphabet.] I. Noyed, Robert B. II. Title.
  PZ7.K6798Dai 2003
  [Fic]—dc21   2003006619

Note to parents and educators:

The first skill children acquire before becoming successful readers is individual letter recognition. The Alphabet Friends series has been created with the needs of young learners in mind. Each engaging book begins by showing the difference between the capital letter and the lowercase letter. In each of the books on the vowels and the consonants c and g, children are introduced to the different sounds that the letter can make. Finally, children see that the letters can be found at the beginning of a word, in the middle of a word, and in most cases, at the end of a word.

Following the introduction, children meet their Alphabet Friends. The friend in each story encounters many words that include the featured letter of that book. Each noun that begins with the title letter is highlighted in red with the initial letter of the word in bold. Above the word is a rebus drawing that establishes a strong picture cue.

At the end of each book, we have included three words lists. Can your young learners find all the words in each book with the title letter in them?

Let's learn about the letter **D.**

The letter **D** can look like this: **D.**

The letter **D** can also look like this: **d.**

The letter **d** can be at the
beginning of a word, like dog.

dog

The letter **d** can be in the
middle of a word, like panda.

pan**d**a

The letter **d** can be at the

end of a word, like food.

foo**d**

I like to do many different things.

I like to play with my **d**og. My **d**og

is named **D**aisy.

I like to draw. I sit at my **d**esk to draw.

I like to draw pictures of **D**aisy.

I like to do things with my **d**ad.

He drives me to the park. My **d**ad

and I play with **D**aisy.

Sometimes I like to dance with my **d**ad.

We dance almost every **d**ay. We do

many different kinds of **d**ances.

I like to dive into the pool. I dive deep to

the bottom. My **d**ad and I dry off in the

sun when we are done. **D**aisy does too!

I like to dig in the garden. It is fun to

dig in the **d**irt with **D**aisy. We get very

dirty when we dig.

I like to do many different things with

my **d**ad and **D**aisy. But when the **d**ay

is done, it is time to lie down.

Fun Facts

Do you know how to **d**ance? Sure you do! Anyone can **d**ance just by moving their body to music. People all around the world **d**ance for different reasons. For example, **d**ance is an important part of some religions. Some people **d**ance as a career. Or you can **d**ance just for fun.

Did anyone ever scold you for getting dirty? You probably didn't know how many kinds of **d**irt there are. Mud, dust, soil, and sand are all types of **d**irt. **D**irt can be made up of rocks, leaves, twigs, dead skin, animal droppings, rotting plants and animals, and even tiny living things. With all that **d**irt, it's hard for a kid to stay clean!

There are many breeds, or kinds, of **d**ogs. The **d**og in this story is a pug. A pug is a small **d**og that has a flat nose, a wrinkled head, and a curled tail. They originally came from China. Pugs are very popular pets.

To Read More

About the Letter D

Flanagan, Alice K. *Dogs: The Sound of D.* Chanhassen, Minn.: The Child's World, 2000.

About Dances

Boynton, Sandra. *Barnyard Dance!* New York: Workman Publications, 1993.

Pinkney, Andrea Davis, and Brian Pinkney (illustrator). *Watch Me Dance.* San Diego, Calif.: Harcourt Brace & Co., 1997.

About Dirt

Cherrington, Janelle, and Joe Ewers (illustrators). *Dirt Is Delightful.* New York: Simon Spotlight, 1999.

Johnston, Tony, and Alexa Brandenberg (illustrator). *We Love the Dirt.* New York: Scholastic, 1997.

About Dogs

Day, Alexandra. *Good Dog, Carl.* La Jolla, Calif.: Green Tiger Press, 1985.

Pilkey, Dav. *Big Dog and Little Dog.* San Diego, Calif.: Harcourt Brace & Co., 1997.

Words with D

Words with D at the Beginning

dad
Daisy
dance
dances
deep
desk
different
dig
dirt
dirty
dive
do
does
dog
done
down
draw
drives
dry

Words with D in the Middle

garden
kinds
middle
panda

Words with D at the End

end
food
named
word

About the Authors

Cynthia Klingel has worked as a high school English teacher and an elementary teacher. She is currently the curriculum director for a Minnesota school district. Cynthia Klingel lives with her family in Mankato, Minnesota.

Robert B. Noyed started his career as a newspaper reporter. Since then, he has worked in communications and public relations for a Minnesota school district for more than fourteen years. Robert B. Noyed lives with his family in Brooklyn Center, Minnesota.